CW00455881

THE SCARLET LETTER

THE SCARLET LETTER

Nathaniel Hawthorne

An imprint of Om Books International

Om KIDZ | Om Books International

Reprinted in 2019

Corporate & Editorial Office
A-12, Sector 64, Noida 201 301
Uttar Pradesh, India
Phone: +91 120 477 4100
Email: editorial@ombooks.com
Website: www.ombooksinternational.com

Sales Office
107, Ansari Road, Darya Ganj
New Delhi 110 002, India
Phone: +91 11 4000 9000
Email: sales@ombooks.com
Website: www.ombooks.com

© Om Books International 2016

Retold by Swayam Ganguly

ISBN: 978-93-85031-65-6

Printed in India

10 9 8 7 6 5 4 3 2

Contents

Chapter One

The Rose Bush

The founders of any new colony realised the importance of allocating one part of their land for a cemetery, and another for a prison-house. In compliance with this rule, one might take the liberty to assume that the first prison-house built by the forefathers of Boston was somewhere near Cornhill. Almost around the same time, they built the first burial ground near Isaac Johnson's grave.

Fifteen to twenty years after the town was established, this prison-house was covered with weather stains that added a gloomy look to its already dull front. The rust that had gathered on the iron spikes of the oak door looked ancient.

Like all that pertains to crime, the prison-house seemed to have never witnessed a youthful era. An overgrown plot of grass lay in between this ugly structure and the wheel track of the street. Here, plants like apple-of-Peru, burdock and pig-weed grew abundantly. A wild rose bush also stood proudly here, almost as if offering its beauty and fragrance to convicts as they were led inside the prison. Only nature could be forgiving in its generosity and beauty to a condemned prisoner.

The huge pines and oaks towering over it fell earlier and died, but this rose bush survived the test of time. Many believe that the rose bush sprang up under the footsteps of the sainted Ann Hutchinson as she walked into the prison-house. We shall not debate this theory, but this rose bush stands directly on the threshold of our narrative. So, we shall pluck one of its flowers and gift it to the reader. It may serve to symbolise some sweet moral blossom to soothe the reader after a dark tale of human vice and sorrow.

One morning, less than two centuries ago, a horde of bearded men, dressed in dull coloured clothes, wearing grey steeple-crowned hats, occupied the grass plot in front of the prison-house in Prison Lane. The door of this wooden prison-house was heavily fortified with iron spikes and timbered with oak. A few women were also present in this gathering. Some women wore hoods while others were bareheaded. All of them stared fixedly at the iron-clamped oak door.

At a later period in New England's history, this grim scene might have signified that some terrible business was about to take place. But, in that early severity of the Puritan character, such an inference could not be drawn so easily. It could have been a notorious criminal being hanged or someone being disciplined at the whipping-post. Perhaps, a stray and rambling native, who had been rioting on the streets under the influence of the white man's fire water, was being chased away into the depths of the forest. Or a witch like old Ann Hibbins was being put to death upon the gallows.

Whatever the case might have been, the solemnity of the spectators would not have differed. For these people of New England, there was hardly any difference between law and religion. Both were so deeply embedded in their characters that for them, the mildest and severest acts of public indiscipline were equally dreadful. If the victim expected sympathy from the bystanders, it was cold and in small measure.

Chapter Two

The Scarlet Letter

Our story begins on a summer morning at the scaffold, where the women in the crowd seemed to take an unusual interest in the punishment that was about to be announced.

The era in which our story is set was not particularly refined and did not impose restrictions on women. They were free to mix around freely with the commoners. These maidens of old English birth were much stronger, both physically and morally, than their fair descendants six or seven centuries later. The women who now stood before the prison-door were countrywomen. They were loud and bold in their speech.

"Good wives," a 50-year-old woman addressed the crowd. "Let me give you a piece of my mind. Won't it be better for the public if mature women like us, who are regular churchgoers, are given the responsibility to handle this evil woman called Hester Prynne? If five of us had pronounced judgment on her, would she have received such an easy sentence as awarded by the magistrates?"

"Even Reverend Dimmesdale, who's her godly pastor, is ashamed of the scandal that she has brought about on his congregation," another woman in the crowd commented.

"The magistrates are too lenient in their judgment," a third matron added. "The least they could have done was to mark Hester Prynne's forehead with a hot iron. If they brand her elsewhere, she might cover the mark with an ornament and still walk the streets proudly."

"She might cover the mark on her body," a young woman, accompanied by a child remarked. "But she will always carry its pain in her heart."

"Why do we talk of silly things like marks and brands?" the cruelest of these self-proclaimed judges suddenly shouted. "The woman has shamed us all and must die! The magistrates will be responsible for not enforcing the law, if their own wives and daughters are led astray."

A man from the crowd exclaimed, "Silence now, gossips. Look, the prison-door is being opened and it is Hester Prynne herself."

The prison-door flung open and the dark figure of the town-beadle ventured into the sunshine, a sword dangling by his side, and his staff of office in the left hand. It was his responsibility to administer the Puritanical code of law, where the offender had to be punished. He laid his right hand on the shoulder of the young woman and drew her forward. But on the threshold of the prison-door, she defied him and walked ahead of her own accord with a dignity of character. She held a baby of three months in her arms. The infant squinted its eyes as they were unaccustomed to the harsh sunlight, having experienced only the dim light of the dungeons before.

The first action of the young woman, when exposed to the crowd outside, was to clutch her infant tightly to her bosom. This was not exactly due to motherly affection as one would assume, but more because she wished to conceal something that was attached to her dress. But she soon realised that one sign of shame would not suffice to hide the other and took the baby in her arms. With a haughty smile, she surveyed the gathering unabashedly.

The young woman was tall, beautiful and a picture of perfect elegance. There was a delicate dignity and grace in her appearance. Her dark and glossy hair reflected the sunshine, and her black eyes were mesmerising. The letter 'A' was artistically embroidered in fine red cloth and decorated with golden thread on her bosom. The crowd was stunned into silence as they looked at her. Her beauty eclipsed her predicament. True, a sensitive eye would have detected the pathos in her eyes, but her reckless spirit was also evident in the way she presented herself. All eyes were

fixed on the scarlet letter that was wonderfully embroidered on her bosom. It was almost as if the letter had cast a spell on the gathering.

"She is very skilled with the needle," a woman complimented. "But has any woman ever displayed it in such a manner as this young hussy?" she demanded. "It seems that her act is meant to laugh on our faces."

"It would serve her right if we stripped her off that embroidered red letter," an old lady hissed. "I'll replace her strange red letter with a rag from my own rheumatic flannel."

"Make way, good people. Make way in the name of the king," the town-beadle declared. "I promise you all that Mistress Prynne shall be led where all of you will be able to see her. Come along now, Mistress Prynne, and display your scarlet letter at the marketplace."

The crowd parted to create a lane through which the beadle led Hester towards the place appointed for her punishment. The crowd followed and schoolboys ran behind her. They

peered into her face, stared at the baby and looked at the shameful letter on her bosom with little understanding of the matter, except that it was a half-holiday for them.

The marketplace was not a long walk from the prison-house, but Hester took some time to get there as she walked slowly. Each step that she took was extremely painful for her. She arrived at the scaffold, which was the platform of the pillory. Above this, constructed in wood and iron, was the instrument of punishment. It would confine the human head in its tight grip and display it to the public. The prisoner could not even hide his or her face in shame.

However, in Hester's case, she had been ordered to stand on this platform and was spared the ordeal of having her head locked into place. She climbed up the wooden steps and stood on the platform. A Papist in this gathering of Puritans might have compared the scene to that of the Divine Mother holding her child. But here, as she stood holding the object of her shame,

Hester Prynne was accused of the deepest sin in the sacred life of mankind. If she had been sentenced to death, no one in the crowd would have protested because of the gravity of her sin.

The important men of Boston, such as the governor and his counsellors were also in attendance. They were either seated or stood in the balcony of the meeting-house, looking down at the platform. In the presence of such august company, the crowd was serious and had no scope to ridicule the matter. As thousands of eyes seemed to burn her under their gaze and stared at her bosom, the unhappy woman tried her best to compose herself. If they had chosen to laugh at her, she would have responded with a sarcastic smile. But this kind of behaviour was sheer torture. Hester wanted to scream out loud.

The memories of her maiden years in this town flashed in her mind. Scenes from the past unfolded in her mind like a play, as she saw her native village in New England first, followed by her old, decaying paternal house. Then she saw her father's solemn face, followed by her

mother's, full of cautious and anxious love. She saw her own face, glowing with girlish beauty, illuminating her reflection in the mirror. Then she saw the face of an old, thin man who looked like some sort of scholar. He was a little deformed, with his left shoulder a bit higher than the right. His eyes were squinted with the effort of reading by lamp light. But those squinted eyes had a gaze penetrative enough to pierce through the soul.

Hester saw the lovely sights of the city of Amsterdam next. A new life had awaited her there, but sadly, it had all crumbled to dust. Suddenly, the present, in the form of the marketplace, returned to haunt Hester as she looked in shock at the faces that stared angrily at her. Was it the reality or a strange dream? She clung to her baby so fiercely that it started crying. Then, she stared down at the scarlet letter and touched it to ensure that the infant and the shame were not a dream. Yes! They were nothing, but her reality.

Chapter Three

The Stranger and the Clergyman

People had eyes only for Hester Prynne. Standing in front of the crowd, with her object of shame in her arms was making Hester extremely uncomfortable. She suddenly felt a sense of relief when she spotted someone in the crowd who could distract her from reality. A native, dressed in his traditional garb was standing in the corner of the crowd. This was not uncommon as natives often visited English settlements. But right next to him, stood a white man, who looked like his companion. This man was dressed in a weird jumble of civilised and savage costume. His face was wrinkled, but he was not an old man.

He looked like someone who had worked on his mental faculties very meticulously. It seemed that he had intentionally selected his clothes to conceal the peculiarity of his body frame. But to Hester, it was evident that one of his shoulders was larger than the other. The figure of the deformed man flashed before her eyes again and she clutched her infant tightly to herself. The baby started bawling in pain, but the mother was oblivious to its discomfort.

The stranger had spotted Hester before she had seen him. His gaze was sharp and penetrative. As he stared at her, a look of terror appeared on his face, like a snake slithering across it. His face darkened with emotion, but he tried to control it. When he saw Hester stare back at him and realised that she had recognised him, the man raised his finger slowly, making a sign in the air and bringing it to his lips. Then, he turned to the man next to him and asked, "Pray, good sir, why has that woman been brought here? What offence has she done?"

"You must be a stranger to these parts, friend," the townsman replied, as he stared at the stranger and his Indian friend curiously. "Otherwise, you would have surely heard about the evil doings of Hester Prynne and the scandal raised by her in Reverend Dimmesdale's Church."

"You are right," the stranger replied. "I am a stranger and a wanderer. I have experienced many dangerous misadventures, both on sea and land. I was held captive by heathen-folk and was rescued and brought here by this native. Will you please tell me more about this woman, Hester Prynne? I hope I've got the name right! What sins has she committed to be brought to the scaffold?"

"Of course," the townsman replied. "Your heart must be glad to escape those lands and be back on a land like godly New England, where the correct punishment is meted out to offenders in front of the public and royal presence. That woman, sir, was the wife of a learned Englishman who had lived for a long time in Amsterdam. But one day, he decided to return to Massachusetts and sent his wife before him. He intended to join her after finishing some business. But no news was received of this gentleman, even though his wife resided in Boston for almost two years. His wife, having been left alone, has committed the most sinful act."

"Aha!" the stranger exclaimed. "I do comprehend now. But the learned man you talk about should have gathered from his books that all this would happen. But who is the father of the child that Mistress Prynne is holding in her arms?"

"That, my friend, is the mystery," the townsman replied. "Hester Prynne refuses to shed light on the matter and the magistrates have given up. Perhaps the guilty party forgets that even though no man knows who he is, God has seen him."

"Maybe the learned man should come forth and solve the mystery himself," the stranger said with a smile.

"If he is still alive," the townsman replied. "Our magistracy is not certain that he is dead as is suspected. So, being merciful, they have decided to spare her life and have ordered Hester Prynne to stand on the platform of the pillory for three hours and wear the mark of shame on her bosom as long as she breathes."

"It's a wise sentence," the stranger declared. "But it hurts me that her partner in crime is still unknown. But he will be known soon!"

Then, he left the marketplace with his native companion. Hester kept staring at the stranger as he left. She had eyes for no one else in the crowd. But somehow, she was relieved to observe him from a distance, instead of interacting with him face-to-face.

Suddenly, a voice from the balcony distracted her attention. Hester looked up and trembled. The voice belonged to the great scholar John Wilson, the most famous and the oldest clergyman of Boston.

"Hester Prynne," he said. "I have spoken with my young brother here, whose sermons you have been privileged to hear." Wilson laid his hand on the shoulder of a young man who looked sickly pale.

"I have asked him to persuade you to reveal the name of the man who has tempted you to commit this sin. He continues to oppose me as he feels that such a confession should not be made in broad daylight, in front of so many people by a woman. But I have convinced him that real shame does not lie in admitting a sin." Wilson turned towards the young man.

"Brother Dimmesdale, what do you say?" he asked. "Will you deal with this poor sinner's soul or shall I?"

Governor Bellingham, who was seated in the balcony, also urged Reverend Dimmesdale to have a word with Hester. All eyes were now focused on the young clergyman.

Reverend Dimmesdale had arrived from one of the famous English universities. He was not only a strikingly handsome man, but also highly respected in his profession due to his eloquence and religious passion. When he spoke, it was similar to an angel speaking from Heaven. Despite his talents, there

was a certain uncharacteristic nervousness in his demeanour. He looked at a loss in front of the crowd and could only be at ease in seclusion. The prospect of speaking to Hester had drained the blood from his face. His lips were quivering.

"Speak to the woman, brother," Mr Wilson urged him again. "Make her confess the truth!"

Reverend Dimmesdale bent his head, praying silently, and then addressed the woman from the balcony, looking straight into her eyes.

"Hester Prynne," he said. "If you feel that it will bring peace to your soul, and your earthly punishment will lead you to salvation, I charge you to speak out the name of your fellow-sinner. Do not be silent out of pity or tenderness for him. If he were to stand beside you on your pedestal of shame, it will be much better than to hide a guilty man for life. Your silence will achieve nothing, except tempting him to become a hypocrite and a sinner. Take this opportunity offered by Heaven to win over the evil and dispel the sorrow within you. Say his name!"

The young clergyman's voice was so powerful that all the listeners were entranced and felt sympathetic towards the young victim. Even the baby held by Hester was affected by the clergyman's speech. It looked towards Reverend Dimmesdale and held up its little arms with a half-happy, half-lamentful babble. The clergyman's appeal was so powerful that people were convinced that Hester would speak the name of the guilty man in no time at all! If she did not, surely, the guilty man himself would come forward and confess to his heinous crime. Neither of the two happened and Hester shook her head in refusal.

"Woman, do not cross the limits of Heaven's mercy," Mr Wilson exclaimed angrily. "Speak out the name so that the scarlet letter can be taken off your bosom."

"Never," replied Hester, not looking at Mr Wilson, but into the troubled eyes of Reverend

Dimmesdale. "The letter is too deeply embedded. It cannot be taken off. So, I shall bear his pain as well as mine!"

"Speak his name so that your child knows a father, woman," a voice from the crowd shouted.

"I will not!" Hester replied, turning pale as death, for she had recognised the voice. "My child shall never know an earthly father and she must seek a Heavenly one!" she declared.

"She will not speak," Reverend Dimmesdale concluded, leaning over the balcony, with his hand covering his chest.

Mr Wilson then launched into a lengthy discourse on sin, referring constantly to the scarlet letter and spoke forcefully for over an hour. The spectators were all moved by his speech but Hester was the least affected. Since that morning, she had endured everything the strongest human possibly could. The powerful voice of the preacher hardly reached her ears and even when she was quieting the baby's

loud protests, she did so mechanically, with little sympathy for the infant. Nothing seemed to affect her now. Hester Prynne was led back to the prison-house. Some whispered how the scarlet letter had glittered to show the way into the dark passage within the prison-house.

Chapter Four

The Strange Physician

After she returned to the prison-house, Hester Prynne was never left unobserved because it was feared that she would attempt to harm herself or her young baby. At night, she became impossible to control, which is when Master Brackett, the jailer, decided to call a physician. Hester's baby was in constant pain and needed more medical assistance than her.

The physician was an expert in Christian medical science. Having lived in the company of natives, he was also familiar with the use of wild medicinal herbs and roots. The physician was none other than the stranger, who had

accompanied the native in the marketplace. This man had been housed in the prison, not for any crime, but for his own safety, till the magistrates met the native chiefs to discuss his ransom. His name was Roger Chillingworth and the jailer was surprised at Hester's silence, when the man entered the room.

Chillingworth requested the jailer to leave him alone with the patient. After the jailer left, he first attended to the child. Once he had examined the baby, he took out a leather case and mixed one of the medical preparations in it with water in a cup.

"My studies in alchemy have made me a better physician than many with a medical degree," he claimed. "But administer the medicine with your own hands as the baby is not mine."

Hester refused to accept the medicine and asked instead, "Would you avenge yourself on an innocent child?"

"You are a foolish woman," the physician replied coldly, but reassuringly. "Why should I harm the child? The medicine will only cure her and I would give the same to my child."

When Hester continued to hesitate, the physician cradled the baby in his arms and administered the medicine himself. After a while, the baby's moans ceased and it was evident that the medicine had worked. It was soon sleeping peacefully. He then examined the mother and as he felt her pulse, she recoiled at the touch that was so familiar, and yet, so cold and alien. The physician then gave her a mixture and asked her to drink it. She took it doubtfully and said, "I have often thought, wished and prayed for death. If Death exists in this cup, so be it!"

"Do you not know me at all Hester? Do you think I'm so shallow that I'd poison you?" Chillingworth enquired calmly. "I'd rather let you live to exact my revenge, so that this sign of shame on your bosom might burn forever," he declared fiercely as he laid a finger on the scarlet letter.

"Drink it," he urged Hester. "Drink it so that you might live in shame forever in the eyes of all men and women, including your husband, who is not the father of your child.

Hester drained the contents of the cup immediately and sat on the bed beside the sleeping baby, while Chillingworth occupied the only chair in the room.

"I will not ask how you disgraced yourself," he said. "It was my fault that I devoted my best years to feed my hungry dream of knowledge. I was also mistaken that intellectual skill could mask physical deformity. If I had been truly wise, as perceived by others, I would have foreseen what has happened. I might have known that, as I emerged from the dismal forest into the world of civilised men, the very first object to greet my eyes would be you Hester Prynne, standing on the scaffold with the scarlet letter on your bosom."

"I was always frank with you," Hester defended her shameful act. "I did not feel any love for you nor did I pretend."

"Yes, I have said that it was my fault," her husband replied. "But till the time I married you, in a way, my life was incomplete. There was no happiness around me. I longed to set up a household and although I was old and deformed, it was not a wild dream. So, I chose to marry you so that I could be comforted by your love. I wanted to take care of you as well."

"I have wronged you greatly," Hester replied.

"Both of us have wronged each other," Chillingworth replied frankly. "I was wrong in assuming that our marriage would be a happy one. I seek no revenge and plan no evil against you. But the man who has done this has wronged us both. Who is he, Hester?" he demanded.

"You shall never know that," Hester replied. "So don't ask me!"

"Never, you say?" he smiled. "Believe me Hester, it is impossible for a man like me to not know something if I set my heart on it. You might hide the truth from the ministers and magistrates, but it shan't escape me. I possess talents that they don't. I shall discover the truth, just like I have looked for gold in alchemy and searched for the truth in books. I shall find this man sooner or later and I shall see him tremble in fear."

As Hester shuddered and covered her heart in fear, her husband continued, "Although he is not branded with the scarlet letter like you, I shall read his sin on his heart. But do not be scared for him! I shall not come in Heaven's way of retribution and shall let nature take its own course. Neither will I whisper his name to the law. I shall let him live! Yet, he shall be mine."

"Your promises are merciful," Hester replied. "Yet, you sound like a villain."

"I'd request you to keep my secret, just like I have kept it a secret that you are my wife," Chillingworth continued. "No one in this land knows me and I'd like to keep it that way. So never tell anyone that I was ever your husband. You still belong to me, Hester, so do not betray me!"

"But why?" she asked. "Why not announce it openly and then cut all ties with me?"

"I shall not be called the husband of a faithless woman," he replied. "Besides, it is my intention to live and die anonymously. So, let your husband be dead like the world assumes. If you do not do

this, beware! The life of the man you love will be in my hands. So beware!"

Hester swore that she would keep his secret just like she had kept the other man's.

"How does it feel to wear the scarlet letter, even in your sleep? Does it bring nightmares?" he asked.

"Why do you taunt me so?" she asked. "Are you the Devil that haunts us all? Have you tied me into a bond that will ruin my soul?"

"Not your soul!" Roger Chillingworth replied.

Chapter Five

Hester's Art

Hester Prynne's prison term ended soon and she was released. When she was exposed to freedom and sunshine, she could sense the entire mankind pointing to the letter branded on her bosom. Hester had only two choices; to either succumb to the ordeal or rise above it. But with each day, her misery only seemed to increase.

Hester could have easily left for any other European country and led a new life there, away from the glaring eyes of people. But she chose to reside in New England with her token of shame. The hope that she might be reunited with the man who had caused her so much grief might have

been another reason why she chose to stay on in New England. Also, Hester was brave enough to admit that if she had sinned, she would stay on this very land and be punished, instead of escaping from her fate.

So, Hester chose to reside on the outskirts of the town, away from other inhabitants. She lived in a small, abandoned cottage, facing the sea, with forests covering the hills towards the west. The magistrates still kept an eye on her and so did the children, who crept up to watch her working with her needle at the cottage window or in her garden. They would then scamper away in fear after spotting the letter.

Although Hester had no friends, she had everything she needed. She was capable enough to produce food, both for herself and her baby, even on land that had been deemed infertile. She was also good with the needle and talented in art. Soon, Hester Prynne's handiwork became the fashion and her needlework began to adorn the Governor's ruff and the scarves of military

men. From a baby's cap to coffins of the dead, her needlework could be seen everywhere. But her so called 'sinful hands' were never called upon to design the white veil of a bride. This notable exception proved that society still looked down upon her.

Hester was not greedy; she could have exploited her skills and made a lot of money, but she was satisfied in earning an amount that took care of herself and her baby's needs. She dressed simply, with the exception of the scarlet letter of course, which she had been doomed to wear for life. She dressed her little girl fancifully in comparison, but apart from this one indulgence, Hester lived her life simply. Instead, she chose to dispense a lot of her new-found wealth in charity, to people who were less fortunate than herself. She spent her spare time in designing clothes for the poor, who were not ungrateful to the sinful hands that fed and clothed them.

What made Hester's art special was its Oriental quality, which was exceptionally singular in its beauty. The toil of the needle is often pleasurable to many women, but to Hester, it was not only an act of expression, but also her only way of expressing and therefore soothing, the anguish in her life. In this way, Hester performed her role in the world and although she had been shunned by society, it did not shake her spirit. During her interactions with the people of the town, not once was Hester made to feel that she really belonged to the society. The society needed her talent, but it did not need her!

Hester had conditioned herself well, and she never responded when she was attacked or insulted verbally. Whenever she went to Church, the text of the discourse revolved around sin and penance. Parents had told their children that there was something sinful and evil about Hester. So they chased her, keeping at a distance, and shouted unmentionable words. Hester always felt eyes prying on the scarlet letter and her agony intensified.

'Had she sinned alone?' she wondered.

This thought would often cross Hester's mind. Although, she was the one branded with the scarlet letter, she was sure that there were many others in society who had committed similar sins, yet escaped the same fate.

Chapter Six

Pearl

Over the years, Hester Prynne's daughter grew up to be a beautiful and intelligent young girl. She was named Pearl by her mother to signify the treasure that she was to her. Hester was convinced that her act had been sinful and therefore, she had no faith that the result would be good. She watched her child grow, fearful that something dreadful or peculiar would happen to her, but the child was perfect in every manner. She had no physical defects. The child had a certain elegance, which is not always found in every girl who is beautiful. Dressed in finery, Pearl looked like a princess living in an isolated cottage.

Due to the terrible ban imposed on her mother, Pearl could not mingle freely in society. This created a problem when she reached an age when social interaction was necessary. She realised that she could not interact with other children or take part in their activities, a strange situation for a young child. But what surprised Hester was that Pearl never tried to make friends with other children when she saw them playing. She refused to talk to them when spoken to and when they insisted, she would throw stones at them and mutter incomprehensible words, resembling a witch's alien language.

Instead of real friends, Pearl made imaginary ones from the unlikeliest of materials. Her playmates, which comprised a stick, a rag and a plant or a flower in the garden, were rather unusual. She spoke in a variety of voices on behalf of those playmates, displaying her creativity. Hester grew increasingly dispirited when she observed Pearl playing like this alone, but the little girl would always smile and continue playing.

A peculiar thing about Pearl needs to be mentioned here. The very first thing that Pearl noticed as a baby was not her mother's smile like most infants do. In fact, the scarlet letter on Hester's bosom was the first thing that caught her eyes. She had grabbed at the embroidered letter as Hester had leaned over her cradle. In a moment of agony, Hester had taken Pearl's hand away from the letter. She had never known a moment's peace after that incident. Pearl might not stare at the scarlet letter for weeks, but when she did, it would be a piercing gaze with a strange smile and an odd expression on her face.

One day, Hester thought that she spotted another face in the black mirror of Pearl's eyes. It was a Devil-like face, full of malice, smiling. The face resembled features that were familiar to Hester once, without the smile and malice. This image stayed with Hester and it tortured her many times later, though less vividly. Then, one afternoon, Pearl chose to collect a bunch of wildflowers and started throwing them one

by one at her mother's bosom, aiming for the scarlet letter. She danced up and down like an elf whenever she managed to hit the letter.

Hester's first impulse was to cover the scarlet letter with both hands. But she gave up and sat, pale as death, looking sadly into Pearl's wild eyes as the flowers rained on her bosom, each wounding her more than the previous one. When Pearl was exhausted, she stared at her mother.

"Child, who are you?" Hester cried.

"I am your little Pearl," the child replied.

"You are not my child," Hester stated, half-playfully. "You are no Pearl of mine. Who sent you here?"

"You tell me, mother," the child approached Hester, looking at her seriously.

"Your Heavenly Father sent you here," she replied hesitantly, and this did not escape the observant Pearl. She touched the scarlet letter suddenly and declared, "He did not send me here. I have no Heavenly Father!"

"Hush, Pearl!" Hester exclaimed. "You must not speak like that. The Heavenly Father sent us all here. Where else did you come from then, you elfish child?"

"You must tell me that, mother," Pearl stated as she laughed and danced on the floor now. Hester was suddenly gripped by a strange doubt and shuddered. Was Pearl really a demon child? She had overheard some townspeople discuss about them. They had been gossiping about how demon children had come to earth. Such children were a result of the sins of young women, and came on earth to achieve their evil purposes. Did Pearl really belong to that hellish breed?

Chapter Seven

The Minister and Pearl

One day, Hester visited Governor Bellingham's mansion to deliver a pair of gloves that he had ordered. Another important reason for her visit was that she had heard rumours about the magistrates conspiring to separate her from Pearl for the general welfare of society. These citizens argued that if Pearl was truly of demonic origin, she must be separated from her mother. If not, it would only do the child good to be taken away to better guardianship.

Little Pearl accompanied her mother to the Governor's mansion. She was dressed beautifully in a crimson velvet tunic. It looked like the scarlet

letter had suddenly come to life! Knowingly or unknowingly, Hester had dressed up Pearl in shades of scarlet. The street children they passed by threw mud at them, but they fled as soon as Pearl charged angrily towards them.

They reached the Governor's mansion, a large wooden house that looked very cheerful. Fragments of broken glass were embedded abundantly in the walls. They glittered like diamonds when the rays of sun fell on them. This dazzling sight delighted Pearl and she started dancing happily.

"You must collect your own sunshine, dear Pearl. I have none to offer you," Hester replied when Pearl asked for the sunshine.

As Pearl and Hester waited for the Governor, the child's attention was attracted by a suit of armour. The helmet and breastplate of this suit was brightly polished, and a fascinated Pearl stared into the mirror of the breastplate.

"Look, mother! I see you here," she exclaimed, and Hester saw that the scarlet letter was reflected

in gigantic proportions and dominated her reflection in the mirror. In fact, as Pearl pointed, smiling her elfish smile, the scarlet letter obscured Hester completely. This made Hester extremely uncomfortable and she led Pearl away from the mirror to the garden. Here, Pearl, spotting the roses started crying for one. Hester tried to quieten her quickly as she heard the Governor approach. Disdainful of her mother's efforts, Pearl screamed wildly first, and then became silent out of curiosity, looking at the strangers who approached.

Governor Bellingham was giving a guided tour of the estates to his visitors. The party comprised minister John Wilson, Reverend Arthur Dimmesdale and physician Roger Chillingworth. Roger Chillingworth and Arthur Dimmesdale had become good friends since the former had successfully treated the clergyman when he had fallen ill.

The Governor walked ahead to throw open the curtains of the huge hall window. The shadows

hid Hester partially from view, but the Governor's eyes fell on little Pearl.

"What do we have here?" a surprised Governor Bellingham asked. "How did such a little guest enter my hall?"

"Why, she's a little bird of scarlet plumage," good old Mr Wilson exclaimed. "Are you an elf or a fairy?" he asked Pearl in jest.

"I am my mother's child," she replied. "My name is Pearl!"

"Pearl, did you say?" the old minister said, trying to pat Pearl on the cheek. "Ruby or red rose I'd have thought. But where is your mother?" he enquired and suddenly spotted Hester. "Ah, I see, this is the same unfortunate child we spoke about," Mr Wilson declared to the Governor and drew the attention of others towards Hester.

"She has arrived at a good time," the Governor remarked as he ushered his guests inside. "We shall discuss the matter now."

The Governor addressed Pearl's mother gravely, "Hester Prynne, much has been spoken

about you lately. We, who are in authority and charge of affairs, have discussed the matter about your child being raised properly by someone other than you. She should wear sober clothes, be disciplined and taught the truths of Heaven and earth. What can you do for the child in this regard?"

"I can teach my little Pearl what I have learnt from this," Hester replied, pointing to the scarlet letter.

"That is your badge of shame, woman," the Governor stated. "It is because of that sign of dishonour that we wish to transfer your child to better hands."

Governor Bellingham requested Mr Wilson to inspect the child and assess if she held the right Christian beliefs for a girl her age. Pearl was unaccustomed to strangers and as the old minister tried to bring Pearl closer to him, she fled. This surprised Mr Wilson because he was usually good with children.

"Can you tell me who made you, Pearl?" he asked. Pearl knew the answer as Hester had instructed her daughter well. But just like other naughty children, she chose not to answer the

old minister's questions at that time. After a long time, Pearl finally replied that no one had made her, and that her mother had merely plucked her off a rose bush. This fantasy had probably come to Pearl's mind when she had seen the red roses in the Governor's garden. The Governor was aghast at Pearl's response. He commented that it was shameful that a girl of three could not tell who had made her and that no further enquiries were required. Hester held her daughter close to her.

"God gave me this child!" she declared. "And in return, he took everything away from me. She is my happiness as well as my torture. You will have to step over my corpse to take her!"

In desperation, Hester turned to Reverend Dimmesdale and requested him to speak on her behalf as he had been her pastor and was more sympathetic than the other men. The young clergyman stepped forward quickly, although he was very nervous. His heart pained at her plight.

"What this woman says is right," he declared. "God has given her this child as well as the

knowledge to control her strange behaviour."
Reverend Dimmesdale kissed Pearl's brow. She
laughed and exited the room.

"That little girl has witchcraft written all over
her," Mr Wilson commented.

"She's a strange child indeed," Chillingworth
remarked. "Is there any way to guess who her
father is?"

"No," Mr Wilson replied. "It is better that the
secret is revealed naturally."

A relieved Hester left the Governor's house
accompanied by Pearl, and as they descended
down the steps, the window upstairs was thrown
open to reveal Mistress Hibbins. She was the ill-
tempered sister of Governor Bellingham, and was
declared a witch a few years later.

"Will you accompany us to the forest tonight?"
she hissed to Hester. "There will be jolly company
and I promised the Black Man that Hester Prynne
would come." By the Black Man, she was referring
to none other than the Devil.

"Please excuse me as I have to take care of my little Pearl," Hester replied smilingly. "If they had taken my Pearl away from me, I would have gladly accompanied you and signed the Black Man's book with my blood."

Chapter Eight

Roger Chillingworth

Roger Chillingworth had promised himself that his old name would never surface again. The sight of Hester Prynne's humiliation at the marketplace had forced him to change his name to Roger Chillingworth and present himself as a physician. Since he was proficient at his work, he was readily accepted because skilled men were rare in the colony. He proved his merit when the young clergyman, Dimmesdale's health deteriorated. He recovered quickly after being treated by the mysterious Chillingworth and soon, the physician became Dimmesdale's medical advisor and he, Chillingworth's pastor.

It was a rare alliance of religion and science and the two became good friends. The two cultivated minds began spending a lot of time together, discussing important matters. Often, one was the guest of the other.

Soon, Dimmesdale's friends made an arrangement by which the two lived in the same house. This way, the physician could keep a constant check on the well-loved clergyman's health. The new house chosen for the two friends belonged to a religious widow who hailed from a respected family. The motherly widow divided the house into two apartments for the convenience of the two friends. The residents of the colony were very happy with this arrangement for their beloved clergyman. They were grateful that he was being well taken care of. But soon, strange rumours began doing the rounds.

An old handicraftsman, who was a resident of London 30 years ago, at the time of Sir Thomas Overbury's murder, recalled having seen the physician before. Sir Thomas Overbury had been

poisoned in the Tower of London on the orders of the Countess of Essex, and a bogus doctor called Dr Forman had been the co-conspirator with the Countess in the murder. What was really suspicious, was that Roger Chillingworth, under a different name then, had been seen in the company of Forman by the old handicraftsman.

Two or three people swore that they had seen Chillingworth in the company of priests involved in black magic. Many also confirmed that Roger Chillingworth had changed drastically as a person, ever since he had moved in with the Reverend Dimmesdale. Earlier, the physician had been calm and studious, but now, there was something inexplicably evil about his face. According to a rumour, an accidental fire, allegedly fed with infernal fuel, had been ignited in his laboratory. It was concluded that the smoke from this fire had affected his personality. People gossiped that he was Satan's messenger who had befriended Reverend Dimmesdale to corrupt him. They hoped and prayed that the clergyman

would emerge victorious from the battle with Satan's emissary. However, they were also sad about the immense mortal agony that he'd have to endure on the path towards his triumph.

Meanwhile, Roger Chillingworth had embarked on an investigation to determine who the father of Hester's child was. It had developed into a consuming fascination that had gripped all his senses. He now dug into the deepest recesses of the young clergyman's heart, just as a miner searches for gold. When Reverend Dimmesdale would grow suspicious and fearful, Chillingworth would become silent.

One day, Reverend Dimmesdale saw Chillingworth examining a bunch of ugly plants and enquired where he had got them from.

"Near the graveyard," the physician replied, as he often used wild plants and weeds to create potent drugs. "These are new to me however, and I discovered them growing on a grave without a tombstone. In fact, these ugly weeds were the only memorials on the grave. Perhaps, they

emerged from the man's heart and grew over his grave to symbolise the dark secret that had been buried with him, what he should have confessed in his lifetime."

"Maybe he wished to do so but could not," Reverend Dimmesdale replied.

"But why not?" the physician asked. "Can't you see how important it is to confess one's sins? It is the power of nature that has made these black weeds grow out of the man's heart, almost as if to demonstrate the dark confessions of his crime."

"That is nothing but your fantasy," the clergyman replied. "There is no power except the Divine Mercy that can extract a confession from the heart of a human being. The hearts which hold such secrets that you speak of will only reveal them to the world when the time is right and not before that. Those secrets shall be revealed in due course, to discover the solutions to the problems that plague mankind, and when they are finally revealed, they shall be done without reluctance and with an uncontrollable joy. "

"Why not reveal them now?" the physician asked quietly. "Why shouldn't the guilty be relieved instantly by their confessions?"

Reverend Dimmesdale appeared to be in great pain as he clutched at his heart, and replied that he had met many who had confessed their secrets to him and were happier once they had done that.

"But many take their secrets to the grave," Chillingworth stated.

"Yes," Reverend Dimmesdale replied. "But these men only appear happy on the outside and are shattered within. It can only worsen things."

"These men deceive themselves," Chillingworth said forcefully, gesturing with his forefinger. "They refuse to claim the shame that belongs to them with the poor excuse of serving God and their fellow-men."

"I would rather speak about the subject of my health," Reverend Dimmesdale said, trying to change the topic as his friend seemed agitated.

Their conversation was suddenly interrupted by the wild laughter of a young child and through the window, they spotted Hester Prynne and her daughter passing by. The little girl was dancing on the graves, while her mother was trying to dissuade her from doing so. Then, she decorated her mother's scarlet letter with prickly burrs picked from the graves.

"That child does not appear human," Roger Chillingworth observed. "The other day, I saw her spray the Governor with water. Is she totally evil? Is she capable of any good deeds?"

Pearl had heard their voices at the window. She looked up and flashed a naughty smile. Then, she threw a prickly burr at the clergyman. The frightened Reverend Dimmesdale ducked nervously as the harmless missile came flying towards him and Pearl clapped her hands in glee. Hester looked up, and the two parties studied each other silently. Then, Pearl laughed loudly and declared, "Come along mother or that old man will catch you, just like he has caught the clergyman. But he cannot catch little Pearl!"

Pearl led her mother away, skipping and dancing on the graves as they went.

"That woman, Hester Prynne, despite her faults, does not seem to hold any secrets in her heart," Chillingworth said. "Do you think she's less miserable because of the scarlet letter on her bosom?"

"There is always a look of pain on her face," Reverend Dimmesdale replied. "But I think it is better for someone who is suffering to display the pain, like this poor woman Hester, rather than hold it all inside the heart."

"You asked me about your health a while ago," the physician said after a pause. "Your disorder is a strange one, but you are not so sick that a good physician can't cure you. Your disease is something that I seem to know, yet know not."

"You speak in riddles, sir," the clergyman exclaimed weakly.

"Well, then," Chillingworth stated. "Do I know everything that I need to know about your ailment as your physician? A bodily disease is often a result of the wound inflicted on the mind. Perhaps, you would care to reveal to me what troubles your soul."

"Not to an earthly physician," Reverend Dimmesdale exclaimed as he rose from his chair and looked at Chillingworth fiercely. "If it is a disease of the soul, I shall share it only with the Almighty. Who are you to meddle in my affairs? Who are you to come between the sufferer and his Heavenly Father?"

Reverend Dimmesdale left the room and Chillingworth smiled behind him.

'It is good that I took this step,' he thought. 'Nothing is lost. We shall be friends again soon, I'm sure. But how the man is moved by passion! I'm certain he has done wild things in passion.'

Reverend Dimmesdale realised after spending some time alone that he had been rash in his behaviour. He apologised to Chillingworth, and they reconciled their differences. One day, at noon, Reverend Dimmesdale fell asleep while reading. This was highly uncharacteristic of him. To add to that, he was sleeping soundly. Soon, Roger Chillingworth came to his room.

He advanced towards him, and moved his shirt aside to inspect his chest. Reverend Dimmesdale stirred slightly in his sleep.

After some time, Chillingworth turned away. He had a look of amazement, joy and terror on his face. He lifted his arms towards the ceiling and stamped his feet on the floor in sheer ecstasy.

Chapter Nine

The Physician's Revenge

After this incident, the dynamics of their equation changed drastically. Roger Chillingworth now had his intentions clear. He planned to exact a terrible revenge on his enemy. Like a magician waves his wand, now, he could make Reverend Dimmesdale miserable whenever he wanted to. While Reverend Dimmesdale had a feeling that some evil influence was following him, Chillingworth performed with such perfect subtlety that he had no idea of the actual nature of the evil.

Due to his illness, Dimmesdale's popularity increased, even though some of his fellow-clergymen

were more deserving than him in his present condition. The public adulation was such that Reverend Dimmesdale was considered a messenger of God. In their eyes, the ground on which he walked was holy. They wanted to be buried next to his grave when death approached them.

'Will the grass ever grow on my cursed grave?' Dimmesdale wondered all this while. Strangely, the clergyman began to despise this public veneration. It was a torture for him.

One day, he addressed the people from the pulpit and told them that he was the worst of the sinners in the world. But this confession only made the people revere him more. They referred to the young clergyman as 'the true saint on earth.'

The clergyman felt worse and loathed himself. He felt like a hypocrite in his own eyes. He had tried to speak the truth but all he had managed was to falsify it. He was ashamed of himself and hated his very existence now.

Reverend Dimmesdale began to engage in practices which were more in tune with the old, corrupted Roman faith than the shining light of the Church where he had been born and raised. He began to fast, but not in a way that purified the body of most holy men. It was torturous and a punishment for the body and the mind.

This fasting was an act of penance, which continued until his knees started trembling. He stayed awake night after night, sometimes in front of a lamp and sometimes in total darkness. He saw demonic visions in this weak state. From angels flying upwards sadly, to his friends who had died, he saw them all. He also saw his parents. His saint-like father had a frown on his face and his mother looked at him with pity. Then, the figure of Hester Prynne glided in, holding her daughter Pearl dressed in her scarlet dress. She pointed to the scarlet letter on her bosom with her forefinger and then pointed it accusingly at Dimmesdale. The clergyman knew

that these visions were not real. But they were the only things that seemed to demand his attention and time.

For the man who has committed a sin, the entire world becomes false. That man becomes a mere shadow of his self. The only reason that continued to give Reverend Dimmesdale an existence was the anguish in his soul.

On one such night, a new thought struck Reverend Dimmesdale. He thought he might find peace if he performed this action. He dressed carefully, walked down the staircase softly, opened the door and stepped out in the dark night.

Chapter Ten

The Vision in the Sky

Reverend Dimmesdale walked like a somnambulist to the platform in the marketplace where Hester Prynne had received her punishment. The clergyman went up the steps and stood on the platform. The town was asleep and there was no fear of discovery. He could stand there all night if he chose to.

'Why have I come here', he wondered. Were the angels miserable and the demons rolling in diabolic laughter?

Crimes were only committed by men with nerves of steel. So how was it possible that a weak man like him could be a criminal?

As he stood on the scaffold, Reverend Dimmesdale was suddenly gripped with immense terror. He felt that the entire universe was staring at the scarlet token on his chest. He cried out loud in pain and his scream reverberated throughout the town.

'There!' he thought. 'That will wake up the whole town and they shall find me here.'

But no such thing happened. His cry was loud only for his own ears and did not wake up the town. If at all anyone heard his scream, they mistook it to be a nightmare or the noise made by Satan's witches as they travelled in the air.

The clergyman spotted Governor Bellingham standing with a lamp on one of his chamber-windows. It was obvious that he had heard the scream. He also saw old Mistress Hibbins, the Governor's sister, on another window. She looked disappointed that the cry did not belong to the dark companions of night who accompanied her to forest excursions. Mistress Hibbins

extinguished her lamp on spotting the Governor and disappeared. After a while, the Governor also went away.

After some time, Reverend Dimmesdale saw a light approaching him and the figure of Mr Wilson came into view. Mr Wilson had been praying at the bedside of the dying Governor Winthrop, and was now returning home. As he passed beside the scaffold, Reverend Dimmesdale could hardly restrain himself from saying aloud, "A good evening to you Father Wilson. Come up here and pass a pleasant hour with me."

Had Reverend Dimmesdale really spoken? For a moment, he believed that he had. But as the Reverend Mr Wilson continued to walk ahead, it became clear that he had only uttered those words in his imagination. It was a cold night, and shortly afterwards, he felt his limbs becoming stiff. He wondered if he'd even be able to descend down the steps of the scaffold. The town would be amazed to discover him the next morning, standing on the platform, where Hester had stood.

Imagining this situation, the clergyman burst into laughter. A small childish laugh responded to his and he recognised Pearl's voice immediately.

"Is that you Pearl?" he cried into the darkness. "Hester, Hester Prynne, are you there?" he demanded.

"Yes, it is," a surprised Hester replied. "Little Pearl is with me."

"Where are you coming from at this hour?" the clergyman asked.

"I was at Governor Winthrop's deathbed, taking his measurement for a robe. I'm going home now," Hester replied.

"Come up Hester, you and Pearl. You have been here before, but I was not with you," Reverend Dimmesdale requested. "Come up now and the three of us shall stand here together."

Hester silently climbed the steps, holding little Pearl by the hand, and stood on the platform by his side. The clergyman held Pearl's hand and a huge rush of life surged through his body, as if the mother and child had communicated their warmth to him. The three of them formed a chain.

"Minister!" Pearl whispered.

"Yes, my child?" Reverend Dimmesdale said.

"Will you stand here with mother and me till noon tomorrow?" she asked.

"No, my child," Reverend Dimmesdale replied, for with new energy, the fear of public exposure had returned to his heart. Pearl laughed and tried to pull her hand away, but the clergyman requested that she hold his hand a little longer.

"Do you promise to take mine and my mother's hand tomorrow at noon?" Pearl asked him again.

"Some other time, Pearl," he replied. "When?" Pearl demanded.

"On judgment day!" Reverend Dimmesdale replied. Pearl laughed again. Before he had finished speaking, suddenly, a meteor lit up the sky. It resembled a gigantic lamp, and from the doorsteps to the wooden houses in the colony, every visible object was illuminated. And there stood the clergyman, with one hand upon his

heart, holding the elf-like Pearl's hand with the other, in this strange and solemn splendour. The clergyman now looked skywards.

It was common in those days to interpret meteoric appearances as supernatural revelations. Weapon-like appearances in the sky symbolised approaching war with natives and a shower of crimson light indicated pestilence. Reverend Dimmesdale, in his disordered state of mind interpreted the sign in the sky as a giant letter 'A', highlighted in red. The meteor, perhaps, indicated no such sign and it was a figment of his imagination. It was probably his own guilt that caused him to see that letter.

Pearl suddenly withdrew her hand and pointed across the street. Reverend Dimmesdale was perfectly aware that she was pointing at the figure of Roger Chillingworth, who stood a little distance away from the scaffold. The clergyman felt that the meteoric light had transformed Chillingworth's appearance. His face was full of hatred, as he stood there smiling and scowling at his victim. This image was so powerful that it

lingered in the clergyman's mind, long after the light from the meteor had vanished.

"Who is that man, Hester?" a terrorised Reverend Dimmesdale enquired. "I pale at the very sight of him. I fear that man in a way that cannot be defined." Hester remembered her promise to Chillingworth and was silent. But Pearl spoke up, "I can tell you who he is, minister."

Pearl whispered into the clergyman's ears and all he heard was childish gibberish. Even if it did make sense, it was in an alien language. Pearl laughed aloud shrilly.

"Are you mocking me?" the clergyman asked the child.

"You were not bold! You were not true!" Pearl replied. "You did not promise to take mine and mother's hand tomorrow at noon."

By then, Roger Chillingworth had approached the clergyman and requested that he lead him home. Chillingworth claimed he had most probably walked there in his sleep.

"How did you know I was here?" the clergyman asked him fearfully.

"I knew nothing about it," the physician replied. He had been by Governor Winthrop's bedside, trying to ease his pain. He was going home when he saw Reverend Dimmesdale standing here. Finally, the clergyman and physician went home together.

The next day was the Sabbath and Reverend Dimmesdale preached a discourse, which was hailed as the most powerful and eloquent one he had ever delivered. As he descended from the pulpit steps, the clergyman met the grey-bearded Sexton, who held a black glove in his hand. Reverend Dimmesdale recognised it as his.

"This was discovered on the scaffold in the morning," the Sexton informed him. "There is no doubt that Satan stole it from you to make a mockery of your reverence. But as usual, he was blind and foolish. A pure hand needs no glove to cover it."

"Thank you, my friend," a startled Reverend Dimmesdale managed to reply.

"You must handle Satan without gloves now," the Sexton said, smiling. "By the way, did your reverence hear of the omen last night? A great letter 'A' was visible in the skies. We have interpreted it as 'Angel', for good Governor Winthrop was made an angel last night."

"No," Reverend Dimmesdale replied. "I have not heard of it!"

Chapter Eleven

Hester Meets Chillingworth

Hester was shocked to discover the state that Reverend Dimmesdale had been reduced to. His nerves seemed absolutely destroyed. Knowing what the poor man had once been like, Hester felt immense compassion and pity towards him. She realised that the clergyman was the only link she had to the society. She could not ignore his appeal for help against his enemy. Hester concluded that she would help the clergyman. After all, she had a responsibility towards him as the two were bound together by mutual crime.

Time had flown past and Hester Prynne was not the young and resourceful woman as before. Pearl

was seven years old now. The positive thing was that the people in town did not hate Hester as they did before. Since she had not retaliated to the insults and was never hostile, the hatred had gradually transformed into compassion, and in some cases, even love. Hester had lived her life in seclusion admiringly. When calamity had struck the town in the form of pestilence, she had displayed extraordinary commitment and kindness to help those who were affected. Such was Hester's reputation now that many people interpreted the 'A' in the scarlet letter as 'Abel'. It had come to signify a woman's inner strength; Hester Prynne's strength.

The people in power and the wise men recognised Hester's good qualities much later than the common people. For them, it was difficult to get rid of their initial prejudices, which were firmly planted in their hearts. But soon enough, their views and rigid stance became moderate.

Hester had lost most of her attractive feminine qualities. Her luxurious hair had been cut short.

She dressed plainly now. The isolation and seclusion that she experienced had also made her a more mature woman. What troubled Hester was that sometimes, her child was as hostile towards her as the world was. This frustrated her to no end and made her contemplate taking her own life as well as her daughter's. However, when she saw that the clergyman was almost on the verge of madness, it gave her a definite purpose to continue living. This was also because a part of Hester felt responsible for the clergyman's present condition. In her delirious state in the prison chamber, she could think of no other way of rescuing him, except by consenting to Roger Chillingworth's promise. However, her meeting with the clergyman had made her realise the impact of her decision. And now, strengthened by years of hardship, she was determined to redeem her error. Reverend Dimmesdale would surely lose his sanity if she did not help him, but Hester was unable to think of a plan to help him. Suddenly, an idea struck her. She decided to meet

her former husband who now went by the name of Roger Chillingworth.

Years of isolation and selfless work had taken Hester to a higher level, spiritually. She no longer felt incapable of handling Chillingworth. On the other hand, the physician, blinded by his desire for revenge, had stooped to the lowest level of a human being. Hester did not have to wait long for the meeting.

One day, as she walked with Pearl near the seaside, she saw Chillingworth collecting herbs and plants to make his medicines. Hester urged Pearl to play alone by the sea and approached her former husband.

"I wish to have a word with you," she said.

"I am fortunate that Mistress Hester wishes to speak to me," Chillingworth replied. "I hear good news about you. I've heard that the magistrates have been conferring to take the scarlet letter off your chest as a grant of pardon."

"The magistrates are not capable of taking off this badge," Hester replied. "If I am worthy, it will fall off on its own.

"Wear it as you please then," the physician replied. Hester was shocked at his reaction. He had been a calm and studious man before, but now, he seemed to be a fierce and aggressive person, rather guarded in his approach. Although he had aged, there was a certain alertness about him. If one was to describe Roger Chillingworth now, he was the perfect example of a man corrupted by the Devil, both in his appearance and action.

"I want to speak to you about the poor clergyman," she said.

"What about him?" Chillingworth demanded.

"I had made a promise to you when we spoke last," Hester said. "I had promised that I would never reveal to the world the relationship that we shared. But I am bound to break that promise when I see you treat that man so cruelly. You have reduced his life to a living death and yet, you are not satisfied."

"I have devoted more time on this miserable priest than any physician might have ever

dedicated to a patient," Chillingworth defended himself. "One word from me would have landed him in the gallows, but I did not do so."

"Death would have been better for him than the state you have now reduced him to," Hester replied.

"You are right," Chillingworth hissed. "He deserved death more than anything else. But I preferred to gain his trust and exact my revenge instead."

"Have you not avenged it? Hasn't his debt been paid?" Hester enquired.

"No!" Chillingworth thundered. "The debt has only increased." Then his voice became calmer, "I'm sure you remember the kind of man I was before. I was a good and kind man, completely devoted to the pursuit of knowledge. Look at me now! I have become a fiend! Who has made me so?" he demanded.

"I have!" Hester exclaimed. "Why didn't you take your revenge on me instead of him?"

"I have left the scarlet letter to exact my revenge," he stated as he smiled and touched the letter.

"Yes," Hester said. "But now, I must reveal our secret because he must judge you by your true character. I shall not be at peace till he realises why you have done what you did. That will pay my debt to him. Do whatever you wish as there is no hope for him, for me or for Pearl. There's no path out of this dismal maze."

"I almost pity you, woman," Chillingworth admitted admiringly. "If only you had been married to a better man than me, this evil would never have surfaced. I pity you as the goodness in your nature has been wasted."

"I pity you too," Hester replied. "Your hatred has transformed you from a wise man to a fiend. Why don't you try becoming the good human being that you were, for your own sake more than anyone else's? Forgive him and let Heaven decide his punishment. I agree that you have been wronged deeply, but can you not forgive him? Will you deny yourself this act of goodness?" she demanded.

"Peace, Hester," the physician declared sadly. "I have not been blessed with such great powers

to pardon someone. My old faith, long forgotten, comes back to me and explains all our actions and our sufferings. You did plant the seed of evil by your first move and since then, it has all been a dark necessity. You, who have wronged me, are not sinful, and neither am I a fiend. It is nothing but our fate! Let the black flower blossom as it should."

Chapter Twelve

Pearl's Questions

Roger Chillingworth took Hester Prynne's leave and started gathering the herbs and roots. As she gazed at him, Hester wondered what sort of herbs the physician was so keen to gather. Were these herbs poisonous, just like him?

"Oh, how I hate the man!" Hester exclaimed. She recalled him sitting in his study, reading his books many years ago. Such a scene had once made Hester happy, but now, those recollections seemed ugly.

'How could I have ever married a man like him?' Hester wondered. 'He has betrayed me. He has done more harm to me than I have to him.'

Hester now began searching for her child. While her mother had been talking to the physician, Pearl had gone to the water's edge and was playing with her reflection. She beckoned to the phantom in water and when it did not emerge, Pearl went to play with little boats that she made out of birch bark. Then, she began to amuse herself by grabbing a live horseshoe by the tail. She also caught several five-fingers and even put a jellyfish in the hot sun to melt. The naughty child then threw pebbles at some sea fowl, breaking the wing of one bird. But Pearl immediately gave up the game when she saw that she had injured a wild creature. She then concentrated on making a headgear by collecting seaweed, to resemble a little mermaid. Pearl also decorated her bosom by creating the letter 'A' from the seaweed.

"I wonder if mother shall ask me what this means?" Pearl thought aloud.

She spotted her mother looking for her and gladly went dancing towards her.

"Dear Pearl," Hester said after being silent for a while. "This green letter 'A' that you are wearing has no meaning. Do you know the meaning of the letter that mother has to wear?"

"Yes mother," Pearl replied innocently. "It is the great letter 'A'."

"Do you know why mother has to wear this letter?" Hester asked.

"Yes," Pearl replied. "It is for the same reason that the minister always keeps his hand over his heart." Hester turned pale.

"What reason?" she asked.

"I have told you all I know, mother," Pearl replied. "Maybe you should ask that old man you've been speaking with. Perhaps he can tell you. But tell me, mother, what does this scarlet letter mean and why do you wear it on your bosom? Why does the minister always cover his heart with his hand?" Pearl held her mother's hand and demanded earnestly.

Hester knew that Pearl wasn't ready for the bitter truth yet.

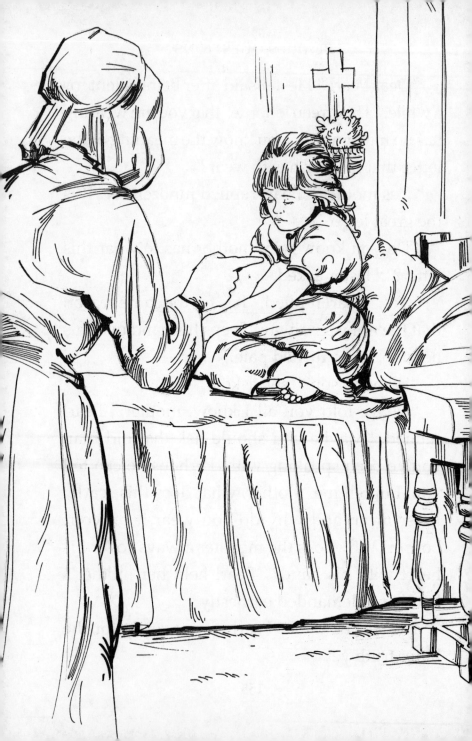

"What kind of questions are these, silly Pearl?" she said. "There are many things in this world that a child must not be aware of. What do I know of the minister's heart? I wear the scarlet letter because of its gold thread."

In all the seven years that had passed, Hester had never been untrue to the scarlet letter. But she had to lie now to Pearl who did not let the matter drop. She kept asking what the scarlet letter meant with mischief glowing in her eyes. The next morning, the first thing that Pearl asked, yet again, was, "Mother! Why does the minister keep his hand over his heart?"

"Hold your tongue, you naughty child," Hester exclaimed. "If you trouble me further, I shall lock you up in the dark closet."

Chapter Thirteen

A Walk in the Forest

Hester made up her mind to tell Dimmesdale about the true character of Roger Chillingworth. She waited for an opportunity to talk to the clergyman on one of his meditative walks in the forest hills or near the sea, but in vain. Had she visited him in his own study, there would have been a scandal. One day, she discovered that he had left the day before to meet Apostle Eliot, who lived with his Indian converts. The next afternoon, when he was expected to return, Hester took Pearl and set off for the forest through which he would enter the town.

It was a cloudy day and there was hardly any sunshine.

"The sunshine is not fond of you, mother," Pearl joked. "It seems to run away from that thing you wear on your bosom. There it is, a long way away. Let me catch it as I am a child and do not wear anything on my bosom yet."

"I hope you never will, Pearl," Hester remarked.

"Why not, mother?" Pearl enquired. "Won't it grow by itself when I'm a woman?"

"Run and catch the sunshine before it disappears," Hester urged her. Pearl ran rapidly and Hester smiled when the child actually managed to catch the sunshine. It glittered on her little face.

"It will go now," Pearl declared.

"Let me catch some of it before it does," Hester said and stretched her hands out. The sunshine disappeared and it seemed that Pearl had actually absorbed it, planning to release some of it when they reached a gloomier area of the narrow forest path.

"Let us rest for a while," Hester urged. Pearl declared that she was not tired, but would rest if Hester told her a story.

"What kind of story?" Hester asked.

"A story about the Black Man," Pearl replied eagerly and mischievously. "About how he haunts the forest, carrying his big, heavy book bound in iron clasps. About how he offers the book and an iron pen to whoever he meets. And how they are supposed to write down their names in their own blood. Then, he sets his mark on their bosoms. Have you ever met the Black Man, mother?" she asked.

"Who told you this story?" Hester demanded.

"The old lady at the house you were last night," Pearl replied. "She also said that old Mistress Hibbins was one of the many thousands who had written their names in blood in the Black Man's book. They all have his mark on them that glows red in the night. Did you meet him in the night too, mother?"

"Have you ever woken up in the night and found me missing?" Hester asked.

"No!" Pearl replied. "But I'd be happy to come with you if you take me. But tell me mother, have you ever met the Black Man? Is this his mark?" she said, pointing to the scarlet letter.

"Will you never bother me if I tell you?" Hester asked. Pearl consented to her mother's demand.

"I have met the Black Man only once," Hester said. "The scarlet letter is his mark." Soon, they heard footsteps coming along the forest path.

"Is it the Black Man?" Pearl enquired.

"No, silly girl," Hester replied. "It is the minister. Go and play while I speak with him."

"Yes, it is," Pearl said as she spotted the clergyman in the distance. "Does he have his hand over his heart because the Black Man marked him there? If so, why hasn't he been marked outside just like you?" she asked.

"Go now Pearl," Hester urged. "But do stay close by."

Pearl left and Hester waited for the clergyman to come closer. He looked pale and haggard. He was leaning on his staff for support. He looked like a man who had lost all zest for life and was holding one hand over his heart.

Chapter Fourteen

The Promise

Arthur Dimmesdale was surprised when he heard someone call out his name in the forest.

"Who is it?" he demanded nervously. He was even more surprised to discover who the voice belonged to.

"Hester Prynne? Is that you?"

"Yes," she replied.

Reverend Dimmesdale extended his hand, cold as death, and caught hold of Hester's. Not a word was spoken as the two sat down. After general conversation about the weather and their respective health, Dimmesdale asked Hester, "Have you found peace?"

She smiled as he stared at the scarlet letter. "Have you?" she asked in reply.

"No," he said. "I have found nothing but despair. What else could I have expected in the way of life that I lead? If I were an atheist and a man lacking conscience, I would have discovered peace long ago. Perhaps, I would have never lost it. But now, all the good things that God has gifted me haunt me monstrously. I am the most miserable man alive, Hester," he confessed sadly.

"But people respect you," Hester protested. "You have done so much good to them, surely it's comforting?"

"It brings more misery," Dimmesdale stated. "How can a man with a polluted soul redeem other souls? People's respect will soon turn to hatred when I confess my sins. I laugh at the thought and Satan laughs with me."

"You are wrong in thinking so," Hester replied gently. "You have repented for your actions and your sin is a thing of the past. The fact that your present life is holy and you are revered by people should bring you peace."

"No," the clergyman protested. "Penance cannot absolve me. Can you ever be happy with the scarlet letter? Mine burns deep within me, secretly, unlike yours. I feel sick when others praise me and I would prefer to be known as the worst of all sinners."

"You have an enemy under your very roof," Hester informed him after a pause. The clergyman clutched at his heart in horror.

"An enemy?" he exclaimed. "What do you mean?"

"Forgive me Arthur," Hester exclaimed. "But I have hidden the truth from you because I had sworn to never reveal it. But now, I must. The old physician living with you, who goes by the name of Roger Chillingworth, was my husband!"

Hester had never seen Arthur Dimmesdale look so furious. But he recovered slowly, only to sink to the ground, burying his face in his hands.

"I should have known it!" he exclaimed. "Somehow, I had guessed it, but I did not comprehend it fully. Oh Hester, you cannot conceive the shame, horror and ugliness of this thing. I shall never forgive you for this."

"You must forgive me," Hester pleaded. "Let God be the one to punish me. But you must forgive me!" She embraced him unexpectedly and begged for his forgiveness.

"I forgive you!" the clergyman said sadly and his anger vanished. "May God forgive the two of us. We are not the worst sinners of them all. The old physician's sin is worse than our sin as he has sought to avenge himself in the cruelest way possible. He has betrayed the purity of a human heart which we have never done."

"No," Hester replied. "What we did had a sacredness of its own. We felt it and spoke about it. Have you forgotten?"

"Hush, Hester," Dimmesdale stood up. "No, I have not forgotten."

The two sat down again, holding hands, on the mossy trunk of a fallen tree. Never had they been as miserable in life as they were now. Though the future looked gloomy for both of them, there was still a certain charm in this meeting. Both of them delayed their eventual journeys back home, just a little bit.

"Hester," Dimmesdale exclaimed suddenly. "Chillingworth is well aware that you intend to reveal his secret. Will he keep our secret then? What new horrors will his revenge unleash?"

"I do not think he will reveal our secret," Hester replied. "He seems to relish the secrecy in exacting his revenge. But he will undoubtedly look for other ways to satisfy his evil passions."

"But how am I supposed to live under the same roof with this strange enemy?" Dimmesdale exclaimed. "Help me Hester!"

"You must not live with him on any account," Hester stated firmly.

"But how?" the clergyman pleaded. "Death seems to be the only way out!"

"The only way is to escape this land," Hester offered. "Go away from the evil Chillingworth. You can travel to London, or even better, to Germany, Italy or France."

But Dimmesdale refused to leave town as he didn't want to escape from his destiny. Although Hester urged him to flee repeatedly and advised him to change his name, he still refused.

"Oh, Hester, you advise a man to run when his legs are giving away," Dimmesdale exclaimed sadly. "I must die here! I do not have the courage or power to venture into this strange world all alone!"

"You shall not go alone," she whispered.

And thus, all was spoken!

Chapter Fifteen

The Scarlet Letter's Curse

Arthur Dimmesdale's face had a look of joy and hope at Hester's statement, but he was also scared and horrified at her boldness. Hester had developed a strength of character after being banished from society which the clergyman was unaware of. She was wild in spirit, just like the natives, while Dimmesdale's actions were regulated by the strict laws of society. The sin that he had committed was of passion, more than anything else, and he had repented it ever since. The seven years of isolation that Hester Prynne had experienced had been the perfect training ground for this very hour. But Dimmesdale was

in the midst of a terrible conflict now. Should he stay or go?

"You will go," Hester declared as if she had read his mind.

Once she had made the decision for him, an inexplicable happiness filled Dimmesdale's heart. It was as if a prisoner had broken free from the shackles of his own heart.

"Let us not dwell in the past," Hester stated as she removed the clasp that fastened the scarlet letter to her bosom. Then, she removed the letter and threw it into the distance.

"See, the past is gone now," she said.

The scarlet letter landed on the edge of the stream, just missing falling into the water. It lay there like a strange jewel, waiting to be picked up by an unlucky wanderer. Hester heaved a huge sigh of relief as her burden was cast away. All her shame and pain vanished. Free from the weight of the scarlet letter, she felt much lighter now. She took off her cap and let her hair loose again. One could see a glimpse of the youth and beauty of

her past. The sunshine chose this very moment to burst forth; nature was at her sympathetic best. Love always manages to create its own sunshine and the forest would have appeared beautiful to both Arthur Dimmesdale and Hester even if it had been gloomy.

"You must know our little Pearl better," Hester said to Dimmesdale. "You must love her as much as I do and advise me how to raise her as she is a little strange."

"But will she be happy to know me?" he asked doubtfully. "Children often distrust me."

"I'm sure the two of you will love each other," Hester declared and called Pearl.

"I can see her now," the clergyman said. "She's standing on the other side of the brook."

Pearl heard her mother calling out to her. She had been playing in the forest where the animals and birds had welcomed her. A wolf had even allowed her to pat its head. Now, Pearl started walking back slowly towards her mother. But Pearl refused to advance further when she

reached the edge of the brook and instead, stared silently at her mother and the clergyman. Hester implored her to come to her but Pearl refused, frowning and pointing her finger at Hester's bosom instead.

"Come here quickly or I shall be very angry," Hester threatened. Her mother's threats infuriated Pearl. She gestured wildly with her finger, stamped her foot angrily and screamed wildly.

"I understand why the child is upset," Hester said to Dimmesdale and she walked to the edge of the brook to pick up the scarlet letter and fastened it to her bosom. Then, she tied her hair back beneath her cap and stretched out her arms to Pearl.

"Do you recognise your mother now, Pearl?" she said. "Will you come to her, now that she is sad again?" Pearl ran into her mother's arms immediately.

"Now, you are my mother and I am your little Pearl," she declared. Pearl kissed her mother in an unusual act of love and then proceeded to kiss the scarlet letter too.

"That is not nice," Hester stated. "When you show me love, you choose to mock me as well."

"What is the minister doing here?" Pearl enquired with curiosity.

"He's come here to welcome you. So come and seek his blessings," Hester replied. "He loves you as well as your mother!"

"Does he love us enough to walk into town holding our hands?" Pearl demanded.

"Not now, dear Pearl," Hester replied. "But in the days to come, he will. We will have a home of our own and he shall teach you many good things and love you dearly. You'll love him too, won't you?"

"Will he keep his hand over his heart always?" Pearl asked.

"What kind of a foolish question is that, Pearl? Come and ask for his blessings," Hester urged. But Pearl refused to make friends with the clergyman. When Dimmesdale tried to win her over by kissing her on her brow, Pearl ran to the brook and washed her forehead, removing all signs of his kiss. She chose to stay away from the clergyman and her mother, watching them silently as they discussed their plans for the future.

Chapter Sixteen

The Minister Recovers

Dimmesdale said goodbye to Hester and Pearl and headed home. He thought about the plans he had made with Hester. They had decided that the Old World was a better prospect for shelter due to its crowded cities, as compared to New England or other parts of America. Luckily, a ship, which had arrived recently from the Spanish Main, was also docked at the harbor and would set sail for Bristol in a few days. Hester was familiar with the captain and crew because of her work as a self enlisted Sister of charity. She thus managed to secure the right of passage for two adults and a child, owing to her goodwill.

The clergyman found the day of the ship's departure most convenient since the day before that he was supposed to preach the Election Sermon, which was a very prestigious event.

'I couldn't have ended my professional career on a better note', he thought.

As he trod along the forest path, Reverend Dimmesdale was full of excitement and positive energy after his meeting with Hester. He met old Mistress Hibbins, the rumoured witch, on the way. She invited him to accompany her to the forest some time at night.

'Have I really sold myself to the Devil whom this old woman considers her master?' the clergyman wondered.

Dimmesdale was lost in thought in his study when Roger Chillingworth arrived, startling him.

"Welcome home!" the physician greeted him and asked him how his trip had been. He also asked him if Dimmesdale needed his assistance to be strong enough to preach the Election Sermon. The clergyman refused and Chillingworth was

sure that he had met Hester Prynne and learnt about the secret. He was certain that Dimmesdale considered him his enemy now. Yet, he insisted that the clergyman avail his services to be stronger for his sermon. But he was refused again politely. Chillingworth had no choice but to leave.

Reverend Dimmesdale had a hearty dinner. Then, he began writing his sermon afresh. He worked all night and till the crack of dawn, he was still writing.

Chapter Seventeen

The New England Holiday

The day the new Governor was to be appointed, Hester arrived at the crowded marketplace with Pearl. It was a public holiday in New England.

Pearl was very curious about the gathering of sailors, natives and other such commoners. She asked her mother why everyone had left their work and gathered in the marketplace.

"They are all waiting for the Governor's procession," Hester informed her. "There will be soldiers marching to the tune of music."

"Will the minister be present?" Pearl asked. "Will he hold out his arms to me like he did at the forest?"

"He will be present," Hester replied. "But today, he shall not greet you and neither should you greet him."

"He is a strange, sad man," Pearl commented. "In the night, he takes our name and beckons us to himself. He talks to you in the forest where only the trees can hear and the sky can see. He kisses my forehead too, but now, in the day and in the presence of so many people, he does not greet us and we must not greet him either. He is a strange, sad man, always with a hand over his heart."

"Hush, Pearl," Hester warned. "You will not understand these things. Do not think about the minister now and take a look around instead. Everyone is so happy about the appointment of a new ruler.

And just as Hester had said, the founders of the commonwealth, the statesmnn, the priests and the soldiers, all came together in a procession to march before the people.

There was also a party of natives standing separately and seriously, dressed in their savage

finery of deer skin clothes, feathers, wampum belts, red and yellow ochre. They were armed with stone-headed spears, and bows and arrows. The rough, fearless and armed sailors from the Spanish Main had also come to watch the procession. These men broke all rules of propriety by smoking in front of the beadle and drinking from their pocket flasks. A townsman would have been fined a shilling if he did that, but a sailor in those days was not bound by such rules. It was also considered dishonourable to interact socially with a sailor. But when a gentleman like Roger Chillingworth spoke on familiar terms with the commander of the vessel, it did not raise many eyebrows.

The commander of the ship was the most well-dressed figure in the crowd. Numerous ribbons decorated his garment and gold lace adorned his hat. A gold lace supporting a feather, was tied around his hat. A sword hung by his side and a wound decorated his forehead. He seemed more eager to display this wound than conceal it. After speaking to the physician, the commander walked

over to Hester Prynne, whom he recognised. The stigma of the scarlet letter had not vanished completely and thus, people maintained their distance from her. This made it easy for her to converse with the commander, without the risk of being overheard.

"I must ask the steward to prepare one more berth than you asked for, mistress," the commander informed Hester. "Don't worry about scurvy or ship fever during this voyage," he assured her. "We have a surgeon on the ship, as well as a physician. There are also medicines I traded with a Spanish ship."

"What do you mean?" a startled Hester asked him. "Do you have another passenger?"

"Why, do you not know of it?" he exclaimed. "This physician called Chillingworth informed me that he was joining your party. He also said that he was a close friend of the gentleman you mentioned and that he was under threat from these Puritan rulers."

"Yes, they know each other well," Hester replied with utmost calmness. "They have lived together for a long time."

That very moment, Hester spotted Roger Chillingworth standing in the assembled crowd, smiling at her. That smile conveyed a dark and sinister meaning.

Chapter Eighteen

The Procession

Before Hester could comprehend this strange new situation and think what to do about it, the sound of military music was heard approaching along the street. It announced the arrival of the procession of magistrates and eminent citizens, heading towards the meeting-house. According to custom, Reverend Dimmesdale would deliver the Election Sermon here.

Soon, the musicians marched into view. There were a variety of instruments being played, tut the musicians were not complementing each other. Yet, they managed to impart a heroic energy to the scene successfully.

Little Pearl clapped her hands and was soon lost in the wonderful scene which was unfolding before her eyes. The sunlight glittered like diamonds on the weapons of the marching army. Prominent citizens, like the magistrates and statesmen, followed the army, marching regally. The priests followed the magistrates and Reverend Arthur Dimmesdale was the cynosure of all eyes. He marched perfectly, without any hesitance. His spiritual strength seemed to carry his weak body gracefully.

Hester felt a deep sense of alienation as she watched the clergyman. He seemed out of reach and so distant now. She felt as if she barely knew him. The dim forest, where they had shared their anguish and made plans for the future, sitting hand-in-hand, seemed like a distant reality now. Pearl seemed to sense her mother's disappointment.

"Was that the same minister that had kissed me?" she asked her mother after the procession had passed by. Hester urged her to be quiet.

"He looked so strange that I was not sure," Pearl explained. "If I was, I'd have run to him and asked him to kiss me again. What do you think he would have done then, mother? Would he have held his hand over his heart and told me to go away?"

"It is good that you did not speak to him, Pearl," Hester replied. "He'd have said that kisses are not appropriate in the marketplace."

Mistress Hibbins, who was infamous for her alliance with the Black Man, had also come to watch the procession. Dressed in a gown of rick velvet, and a gold-headed cane, she now initiated a conversation with Hester.

"Everyone thinks that the young clergyman who went past us is a saint. He certainly looks like one too. Tell me, Hester, did the same man meet you on the forest path?" she asked.

"I don't know what you are talking about madam," Hester replied. "It is not correct for me to gossip about a holy man like the Reverend Dimmesdale."

"Fie, woman!" Mistress Hibbins shook her finger angrily at Hester. "I have been to the forest so many times. Do you think I'm a fool not to know who meets whom there? The Black Man has eyes to see who belongs to him but is shy of joining him. What is it that the clergyman tries to hide by covering his heart with his hand, eh Hester Prynne?"

"What is it Mistress Hibbins?" Pearl demanded eagerly. "Have you seen it?"

"Never mind, darling," Mistress Hibbins replied. "You shall see it sometime. But, they say that you are a descendant of the Prince of Air," she declared to Pearl. "Won't you accompany me some night to fly and meet your father? Then, you shall learn why the clergyman covers his heart with his hand," the eccentric woman declared. She cackled like a witch and everyone in the marketplace heard her laughter.

By this time, the first prayer had been offered in the meeting-house and Reverend Dimmesdale had begun his sermon. Hester listened to him

from beside the scaffold of the pillory. The voice of the clergyman was soothing and everyone listened to him intently. His poignant words touched every member in the audience.

Meanwhile, Pearl was playing alone in the marketplace. In fact, she was upto mischief and the crowd smiled as she engaged in her silly antics. She danced in the company of the sailors, who looked at her in amazement. The commander made an attempt to catch hold of her but failed. He even threw his gold chain to the child. Pearl immediately wore it around her neck and continued to dance.

"Will you carry a message to your mother?" the commander asked Pearl.

"Only if the message pleases me," Pearl replied mischievously.

"Tell her that I spoke with the deformed, old doctor," the commander said. "He will bring the other gentleman on board with him. So your mother should only worry about herself and you. Will you tell her this?"

Before he could complete his sentence, Pearl rushed through the market and communicated the message to her mother. Hester's spirit sank as she could see a huge hurdle in her escape plan. With her mind already troubled, another problem awaited her. There were many people from the country who were curious to spot the woman branded with the scarlet letter. They jostled with each other to get a glimpse of Hester Prynne. Even the sailors and natives joined in curiously and hundreds of eyes stared rudely at Hester, making her very uncomfortable. As Hester stood in the middle of the huge circle that had formed around her, the much respected clergyman stared at the audience that had just been won over by his words. Who would have thought that the honourable preacher and the sinful woman shared the same sin?

Chapter Nineteen

The Revelation of the Scarlet Letter

After the clergyman's eloquent speech came to an end, there was complete silence in the marketplace. After a while, when the crowd was slowly released from the magic spell of his words, it started whispering. They were full of admiration for the clergyman, speaking excitedly as they exited the church. According to them, never had any priest spoken in such a magnificent manner in New England before. Many hailed the clergyman as a prophet of God. But throughout his discourse, Reverend Dimmesdale had spoken in a sad and poignant tone that seemed to indicate

the regret of a man who was to depart soon for his Heavenly abode. It was as if an angel had showered the people with his Heavenly wisdom before departing for Heaven.

Music was heard again as the military directed the procession towards the town hall, where the banquet was supposed to be held. The swarm of people parted respectfully to create a path for the congregation of magistrates and the Governor as they proceeded to the town hall. The crowd cheered them. Reverend Arthur Dimmesdale received the loudest cheers. Despite his triumph, he looked pale and the glow that he had on his face during his sermon had extinguished. He looked like the ghost of the man who had delivered the sermon. Although he walked unsteadily, he did not fall. His old colleague, Mr John Wilson saw the condition Dimmesdale was in and immediately stepped forward to offer his arm for support, but the clergyman politely declined and walked on. He continued walking and his gait can best be described as that of an infant who had been cajoled into walking towards his mother's outstretched arms. The clergyman finally reached the well-remembered scaffold. Hester Prynne and her child Pearl had stood there.

Wilson had kept an anxious eye on the clergyman. He had abandoned his own position in the procession to be close to him to offer his assistance, convinced that Dimmesdale would fall. But something in the clergyman's expression made him stand back. Meanwhile, the crowd, watched his slow progress with wonder. For them, this earthly weakness was just an indication of the clergyman's Heavenly powers. Dimmesdale turned towards the scaffold, stretched his arms forward and cried, "Hester, come here. Come, my little Pearl!"

Although the clergyman stared at Hester and her child with a ghost-like gaze, at the same time, there was also a strange sense of tenderness and victory in his eyes. Pearl quickly ran towards him and held his knees with her hands. Hester followed but stood a little distance away from him. That very moment, Roger Chillingworth burst forth from the crowd, with an evil look on his face. He looked savage, and grabbed the clergyman's hand.

"You madman!" he exclaimed. "What do you intend to do? Get rid of this child and all will be well. Do not darken the sacred fame that you have earned and do not end it all in dishonour! I can still save you!"

"You tempter! You are too late," the clergyman said, looking at him fearfully, but resolutely. "You have no power over me now. I shall escape you with God's help now." Then, he extended a hand towards Hester.

"Hester Prynne," he declared. "In the name of our Lord, who gives me grace at this last stage to do what I have kept myself from doing in seven long years, suffering miserably in the process, I call upon you now. Come here and help me up the scaffold so that we can defeat this poor and wronged man who opposes this act with the fiend's powers."

The crowd was in a state of disorder and the men of prominence, who were standing around

the clergyman, were so surprised that they were rendered silent. Dimmesdale leaned on Hester's shoulders for support and they ascended the steps of the scaffold, together with Pearl, who held one hand of the clergyman.

"Had you tried to escape to any corner of the world, I would have still found you," Chillingworth declared to the clergyman. "The only place where you could escape me was probably this scaffold."

"HE has led me here," the clergyman replied. "So, thanks to HIM!"

"Isn't this better than what we dreamt of in the forest," he smiled weakly at Hester.

"I don't know," she replied. "Perhaps it's best if all three of us die together. You, me and little Pearl."

"Only God can decide about you and Pearl," the clergyman replied. "Remember that only God is all merciful. He has made it clear to me that my time has come. So, let me hasten to confess my shame before I die."

The clergyman turned to the crowd of people

present. "People of New England," he began.
"You have all loved me and regarded me a scared
man, but I am nothing but a sinner! I am standing
on the very same spot where I should have stood
with this woman seven years ago. Behold the
scarlet letter that Hester Prynne wears. You have
all shuddered at the very sight of it. But there is
one more mark of sin that you haven't witnessed
yet." He paused, and for a moment, it seemed that
the clergyman wouldn't reveal his deadly secret.

But he fought back with his last energy to
continue his speech, "God was aware of it and
the angels pointed towards it. The Devil knew
and ignited the mark continuously with his evil
finger, but he cleverly hid it from the knowledge
of the world. Now, at his last hour, the man
with the mark confesses before you all. Look
at Hester's scarlet letter yet again, so that you
might recognise its shadow that he wears on his
own chest. Behold!" the clergyman cried as he
tore open the ministerial band that he wore on
his chest. As the mark on his chest was revealed,

people gasped in shock. Reverend Dimmesdale stood there with a triumphant look on his face. Despite the unbearable pain, he felt that he had won a glorious victory.

Then, he fell down on the scaffold. Hester raised him partially and rested his head against her bosom. Roger Chillingworth knelt beside him with a blank look on his face, as if all life had deserted him.

"You have escaped me," he kept saying.

"May God forgive you," the clergyman responded. "You have sinned deeply too." Then he turned away from the physician and looked at Hester and Pearl.

"My little Pearl," he said weakly, but kindly, as he had been relieved of his great burden. "Will you kiss me now? You wouldn't in the forest, but will you now?"

Pearl kissed him. A spell was broken. The great scene of sadness, in which Pearl had played a vital role, made her cry. Her tears fell on her father's cheek.

"Hester," the clergyman declared. "Farewell!"

"Shall we never meet again?" Hester enquired. "Shall we not spend our immortal life together? Have we not redeemed our sins? You have seen the eternal future. Please tell me what you have seen?"

"Hush, Hester," he replied. "Let the law that we broke and the sin we committed together be the only thing in your thoughts. Our violation makes our everlasting union impossible. But God knows everything and he is merciful! He is the one who has shown his mercy by giving me this mark to wear on my chest. He sent that old physician after me to keep my torture fresh so that I was always reminded of my sin. But he has also ensured that I die a triumphant death by confessing my sin. Praised be his name! Farewell Hester!" These were the clergyman's final words as life left him. The crowd that had been silent till that moment gave a collective gasp of awe and wonder.

Chapter Twenty

Conclusion

After many years, when people of the town would reminisce the incident, various accounts surfaced. Most of the spectators agreed on having spotted a scarlet letter engraved in the chest of the clergyman when he had exposed his flesh. There were various explanations about its origin as well. Some said that the holy man had begun a rigorous penance as soon as Hester Prynne had been sentenced. Apparently, he had tortured his body in many ways to carve an exact replica of the scarlet letter on his chest. Others believed that Roger Chillingworth had caused the mark to appear on the clergyman's body through

his potions and drugs. There were others who suggested that the scarlet letter had appeared on the clergyman's chest as a result of his constant remorse. It is up to the reader to choose from any one of these contradictory theories.

Certain spectators claimed that there was no sign on Reverend Dimmesdale's chest and it had merely been an illusion. The message that the clergyman had imparted before his death was an important one because it indicated that in the eyes of the Almighty, we were all sinners, in one way or the other. He also conveyed that only the holiest of men were able to decipher the divine grace that was showered on mankind. Among the many morals that we can learn from this poor clergyman's sad experience, the most important one would be that no man or woman is free from faults or imperfections.

What was most remarkable after Dimmesdale's death was the change in Roger Chillingworth's character. Apparently, all his powers and energy, including medicinal skills had faded away. When Roger Chillingworth died that very year,

he left behind a large share of his property to Pearl, Hester Prynne's daughter. Pearl became the richest heiress of her age in the New World and was happily married. The story of the scarlet letter became a legend.

Years later, Hester Prynne returned to live in her cottage alone. The scarlet letter never quit Hester's bosom but it was not an object of scorn and ridicule anymore, but of awe and respect. Many troubled women approached Hester for counsel and she did her best to advise and soothe them. Hester was sure that the angel of the approaching revelation must be a woman; pure, wise, beautiful and happy and not enveloped in life-long grief.

Many years later, a new grave was fashioned beside an old, sunken grave. A space was left between the two graves indicating that the two occupants had no right to mingle. Yet, only one tombstone served for both the graves. The letter 'A' was engraved, in red on the black background of a simple slab of state to denote the legend of the scarlet letter.

About the author

■ Nathaniel Hawthorne

Nathaniel Hawthorne was born on the 4th of July, 1804, in Salem Massachusetts and wrote novels like *The Scarlet Letter, The House of Seven Gables* and the short story, *Young Goodman Brown* among others. He was the only son of Nathaniel and Elizabeth Clark Hawthorne. After his father, a sea-captain, died in 1808, the family moved in with Elizabeth's rich brothers to support themselves. A leg injury at an early age rendered a young Nathaniel immobile for many months. He devoted his time to reading heavily and decided to become a writer.

Young Hawthorne attended Bowdoin College from 1821 to 1825. Henry Wadsworth Longfellow and future president Franklin Pierce were his friends here. After graduating, he returned home for 12 long years and devoted his time to serious writing. But writing didn't provide Nathaniel with a substantial income and he worked in the Boston Custom House for a while, weighing and gauging salt and coal. Nathaniel ended his self-imposed exile when he met Sophia Peabody. During their courtship, he frequented the Brook Farm Community where he met Ralph Waldo Emerson and Henry David Thoreau. He married Sophia in 1842 and the couple settled in Concord, Massachusetts, where they had three children.

Nathaniel Hawthorne was forced to move to Salem due to mounting debts. But he lost his job in the Salem Custom House because of political favouritism. This was a blessing in disguise as it gave him time to write his masterpiece, *The Scarlet Letter*, the novel that made Hawthorne famous. He died in his sleep on 19th May, 1864 at Plymouth, New Hampshire.

■ Characters

Hester Prynne: She is the protagonist of the story and wears the scarlet letter, from where the novel derives its title. The scarlet letter is a patch of embroidery, shaped like the letter 'A', which indicates that Hester Prynne is an 'adulterer'. As a young woman, Hester married an elderly scholar who sent her to America, but did not accompany her. She waited for him for years, and then had an affair with a Puritan clergyman, Arthur Dimmesdale, giving birth to a daughter named Pearl. Hester is a passionate woman who also possesses strength of character as she endures shame and ridicule for many years. When she is banished, she puts her exile to good use to reflect on the problems in her community, especially in the way women are treated, and tries to solve them.

Pearl: She is the illegitimate daughter of Hester Prynne and Arthur Dimmesdale. Pearl is naughty, moody and has an elfish spirit. She has an uncanny ability to understand things, which others do not. The townspeople believe that she is not a human child, but the offspring of Devil himself. Pearl is wise beyond her years and often questions her mother regarding the scarlet letter.

Reverend Arthur Dimmesdale: He is a young man who received fame as a theologian in England before immigrating to America. He becomes Hester's lover in a moment of weakness and is the father of her child, although he does not confess this publicly till the end of the novel. He is extremely troubled by this guilt. Dimmesdale is an intelligent and emotional man, and the sermons he delivers are eloquent masterpieces. He's revered and loved by one and all in the society. His dedication towards his profession is in constant conflict with his guilt and the need to confess his sin.

Roger Chillingworth: He is Hester's husband in disguise under this name. He is much older than Hester and had sent her ahead of him to America, while he went on his quest for knowledge to Europe. He was captured by the natives, thereby delaying his arrival in Boston. On his arrival, he discovers Hester and her illegitimate child being displayed on the scaffold. This enrages him and he decides to stay in Boston and exact revenge from the culprit. Using his medical skills, he disguises himself as a physician and swears Hester to secrecy about his true identity. He is determined to discover who Hester's anonymous lover is. Chillingworth is self-absorbed and his sole intention of seeking revenge makes him the most spiteful character in the novel.

■ Questions

Chapter 1
- *Describe the rose bush that grew outside the prison.*
- *What was the rumour about its origin?*

Chapter 2
- *How were the English women of that day and age different from the English women presented in the novel?*
- *What were the memories that flashed through Hester Prynne's mind as she stood on the scaffold?*

Chapter 3
- *Who was the man Hester spotted in the crowd? Describe him.*
- *What did Reverend Arthur Dimmesdale tell Hester? What was her reaction?*

Chapter 4
- *Why did the jailer decide to call a physician?*
- *Describe the conversation between the physician and Hester in brief.*

Chapter 5

- *How did Hester make ends meet when she was forced to live in isolation?*
- *Why was Hester sad with her new life?*

Chapter 6

- *What was the name of Hester's daughter? What were the problems that she faced?*
- *What did Hester fear for her daughter?*

Chapter 7

- *What did the Governor propose to Hester about her daughter? What was Hester's reaction?*
- *Describe the conversation between Hester Prynne and Mistress Hibbins.*

Chapter 8

- *How did Roger Chillingworth and Arthur Dimmesdale become good friends?*
- *Why did the two friends have an argument? Describe in detail.*

Chapter 9

- *What practices did Dimmesdale engage in as a penance to his sin?*
- *What were the visions that the clergyman saw?*

Chapter 10

- *Where did Dimmesdale walk to in the night? Who did he meet there? Describe in detail.*
- *Describe the meteoric appearance that was witnessed in the sky? How was it interpreted by the Sexton?*

Chapter 11

- *How did Hester Prynne win over the townspeople?*
- *Why did Hester meet Roger Chillingworth? What did she request him?*

Chapter 12

- *How did Pearl amuse herself while her mother spoke to the physician?*
- *What questions did Pearl ask her mother? What did Hester reply?*

Chapter 13

- *Who was the Black Man? What story about the Black Man did Pearl narrate to Hester?*

- *Why did Hester and Pearl come to the forest? Explain.*

Chapter 14

- *Describe the meeting between Dimmesdale and Hester in the forest.*
- *What secret did Hester reveal to Dimmesdale? What was his reaction and why?*

Chapter 15

- *Why did Pearl refuse to approach her mother? How did Hester finally make her do so?*
- *How did Dimmesdale try to win over Pearl? What was Pearl's reaction?*

Chapter 16

- *What plan did Hester and Arthur Dimmesdale make?*
- *Why did Dimmesdale approve of this plan?*

Chapter 17

- *Why was a public holiday declared in New England?*
- *What did the commander of the ship say to Hester? Why was she surprised?*

Chapter 18

- *Describe Reverend Dimmesdale's Election Sermon? What effect did it have on the people?*
- *What message did the commander give Pearl to communicate to her mother?*

Chapter 19

- *How did Arthur Dimmesdale confess his sin? Describe in detail.*
- *Describe Dimmesdale's last interaction with Pearl on the scaffold.*

Chapter 20

- *What was the mark on Arthur Dimmesdale's chest? How was it revealed?*
- *What were the various explanations about the mark on Arthur Dimmesdale's chest?*